ADVENTURE AT THE WAX MUSEUM

Madeline Sunshine

SPRINT BOOKS

SCHOLASTIC BOOK SERVICES
New York Toronto London Auckland Sydney Tokyo

**For my mother
with love**

Illustrated by Kye Carbone

This book is from Sprint Starter Library C.
Other titles in this library are:
Space Scooter
Jody
The Shortest Sheriff in the West
Cheap Skates

ISBN 0-590-30974-9

12 11 10 9 8 7 6 5 4 3 2 1   9   0 1 2 3 4 5/8

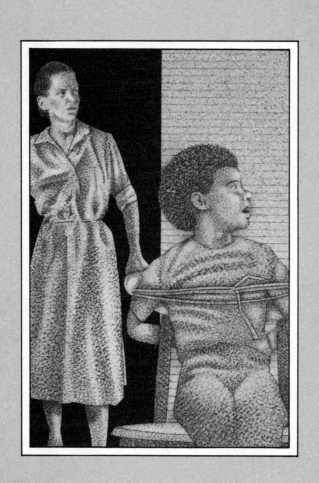

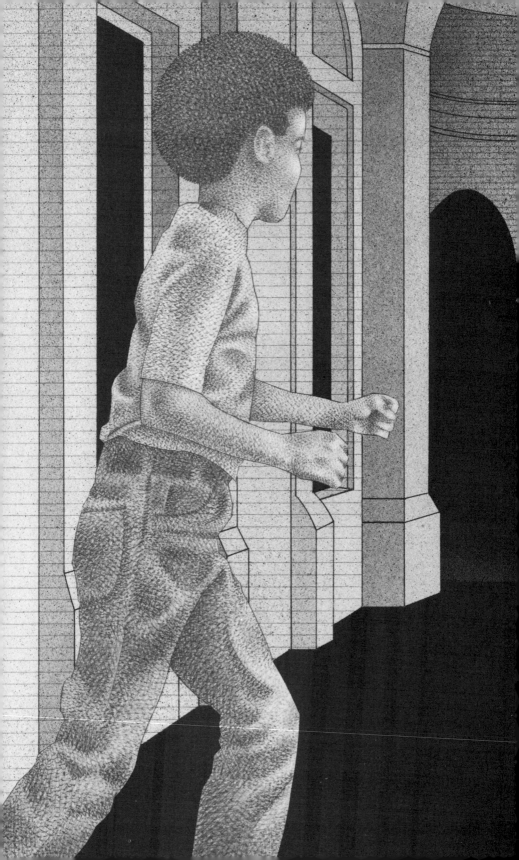

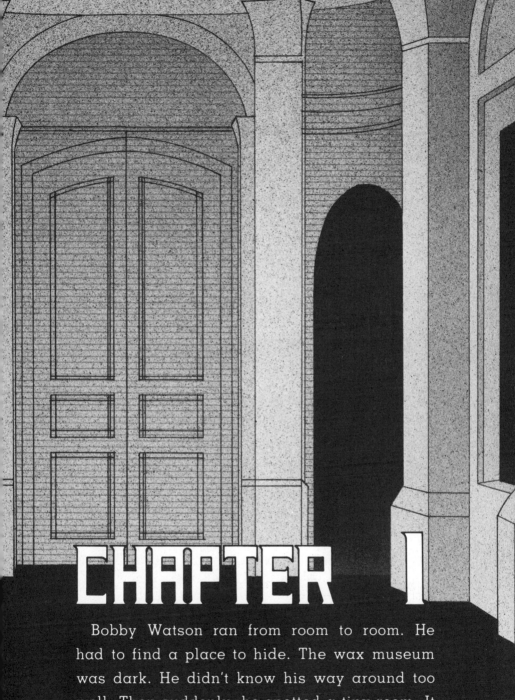

CHAPTER 1

Bobby Watson ran from room to room. He had to find a place to hide. The wax museum was dark. He didn't know his way around too well. Then suddenly, he spotted a tiny room. It was all the way at the back of the museum.

"Mike will never find me in there," Bobby

thought to himself. He rushed toward the room. As he did, he heard a voice call out. "Ready or not, here I come!" Bobby hurried into the little room. He shut the door. Then he sat down and waited.

Hide-and-seek at the wax museum! It had been Mike's idea. But Bobby had agreed at once. It was exciting. It was much more fun than playing outside.

"IT'S THREE O'CLOCK," called a voice over the loudspeaker. "THE MUSEUM IS CLOSING. PLEASE LEAVE THROUGH THE FRONT DOORS."

The announcement was made over and over again. But Bobby never heard it. And he didn't hear his friend calling to him, either.

Soon Bobby became restless. "Why hasn't Mike found me already?" he muttered. "Maybe I found too good a hiding place."

He stood up and walked out of the little room. "Mike," he called. "Here I am." He waited a moment. No one answered. "Mike! Where are you?" He hurried to the front of the museum. Mike was gone. And so was everyone else. Bobby ran up to the front doors. But it was no use. They were locked. He tried the side doors. They would not open, either. That's when it hit him. The museum had closed for the day. And somehow, he had been locked inside.

CHAPTER 2

Bobby looked around. The room seemed to be getting darker. The wax figures threw weird shadows on the walls. He felt as if all the wax statues were watching him.

"I've got to get out of here," he thought to himself. Just then, he saw a sign that said "Telephones." He pulled a dime out of his pocket. He ran toward the sign. But his dime would do him no good. The telephones were in another room. And the door to that room was locked. Bobby pounded on it with his fist. "Open up!" he yelled. "Open up!" Then he ran to the front door. He pounded on it too. Bobby was beginning to panic. "Help!" he cried. "Please let me out!" But no one heard his frightened screams.

Suddenly, he thought he saw something move. He wheeled around. But there was nothing there.

"Cut it out," he told himself. "You are scared enough. Don't start imagining things."

Bobby found a bench and sat down to think. He closed his eyes for a moment. When he opened them again, he saw a short figure dashing by him.

"That's not my imagination," he thought. "That's a real person."

"Wait!" he screamed out. The man turned and looked at Bobby. Then, without a word, the man began running again. Bobby jumped up and rushed after him. But he was not fast enough. The man disappeared. "What's going on?" he cried. "How could that man have disappeared?"

Suddenly, Bobby felt a hand on his shoulder. "Elementary, my dear Watson," a strange, deep voice whispered in his ear.

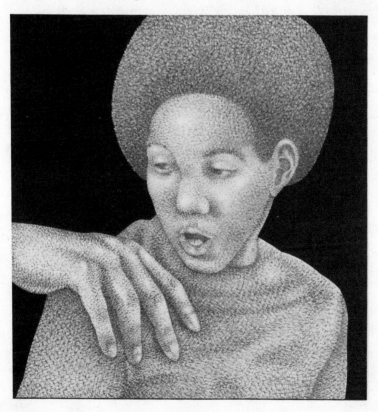

CHAPTER 3

Bobby spun around. He was met by a puff of smoke. When the smoke cleared, he saw a tall man. The man was wearing a hat and cape. Hanging from his mouth was a pipe.

"Who are you?" Bobby cried. "And how did you know my last name?"

"I'm Sherlock Holmes," the man replied. "The greatest detective of all time! Learning your name," he added, "was elementary. I heard your friend calling to you earlier."

"But you can't be real," said Bobby. "I saw you in the other room. You were made of wax."

"So I was," said Sherlock. "But there has been a jewel robbery. And without me, the police will never get their man. Only you and I have seen his face."

"I saw him?" exclaimed Bobby.

"Yes," said Sherlock. "You were chasing him a few moments ago. He hid the jewels here, on the wax figure of Queen Victoria."

"I don't understand," said Bobby. "How did he disappear?"

"Through the back door," said Sherlock. "I'll show you. But you must help me with this case. I promise, it will be quite an adventure."

"Wow!" thought the boy. "Me and Sherlock Holmes!"

"What do we do first?" Bobby asked eagerly.

"First we find our crook again," replied the man. "Come, let's get started." Sherlock led the way toward the back door. Bobby followed close behind. But the boy didn't look where he was going. He tripped and began to fall. In the dark, he grabbed onto something. It felt like a hand. "Mr. Holmes!" he cried. But before Sherlock could answer, a voice called out, "Freeze! We have you covered. One more move and you are done for!"

11

CHAPTER 4

Bobby screamed. Sherlock began to laugh.

"No need to worry," he said. "The voice you heard came from the statue of Wyatt Earp. You must have grabbed his hand in the dark. That's what makes him talk." Sherlock touched Earp's hand. The statue started talking again. Bobby sighed with relief.

"Now let's get going," Sherlock said. "Our robber is waiting." He led Bobby out the back door.

"But how will we find him?" asked Bobby. "There is a whole city out there."

"Elementary, my dear Watson," replied Sherlock. "He was dressed in a fine suit. He

also wore a lot of jewelry."

"So what?" said Bobby. "Many people wear fine clothes and jewelry."

"True," said Sherlock. "But did you notice the mark around his eye? It was made by a loupe. A loupe is a magnifying glass used to look at jewelry. So, our robber probably works in a jewelry store." Sherlock pointed to a sign across the street.

"Circle Jewelry Store," Bobby read excitedly.

"Exactly," said Sherlock. "That's the store that was robbed. And, that's where we will find our robber."

He and Bobby hurried over to the shop. "Stay close, Watson," Sherlock whispered as they walked inside.

"May I help you?" asked the woman behind the counter.

"Perhaps," Sherlock said. "I'm looking for a man. He is wearing a fine suit and jewelry. He also has a mark around his eye."

"You must mean Mr. Stevens," said the woman. "He's our manager. I'll get him for you." She rushed off to the back.

"See, Watson!" whispered Sherlock. "Pretty clever, eh?"

Bobby didn't answer. Sherlock turned around. "Bobby..." he began to say. But much to Sherlock's alarm, Bobby was gone.

CHAPTER 5

Sherlock looked all around the store. "Oh no!" he thought. "Watson must have been captured."

Just then, Mr. Stevens walked up to him. "You wanted to see me," he said with a cold sneer.

"Yes," replied Sherlock. "I have something to discuss with you."

"Oh, really," said Stevens. "What?"

"The wax museum," whispered Sherlock. "And," he added, "Queen Victoria's new jewels."

Stevens gasped in surprise. "Follow me," he said. He took Sherlock down a stairway. At the bottom, Sherlock grabbed the man from behind.

"OK, my crooked friend," Sherlock exclaimed. "Where is the boy? Take me to him."

"All right," said Stevens. "Anita!" he called out. "Come out here. And bring the boy with you."

Suddenly, the woman Sherlock had seen earlier appeared. She was holding Bobby. His hands were tied behind his back.

"You didn't know there were two of us," she laughed in a nasty way. "Now let go of my partner or the boy gets hurt."

"Don't listen to her," screamed Bobby.

Sherlock admired Bobby's bravery. But he knew he had no choice. He could not let the boy get hurt.

"You win for now," Sherlock said. "But you won't win for long!"

"We will see about that," said Stevens. "I thought the boy was the only one who saw me in the museum. But no matter! I have you both now."

The crooks pushed Sherlock and Bobby into a small office. Then they tied each of them to a chair.

"Anita," said Stevens. "We had better close up the shop. We don't want anyone else walking in on us."

"Yes," the woman said. "And then we will get rid of these two troublemakers for good."

19

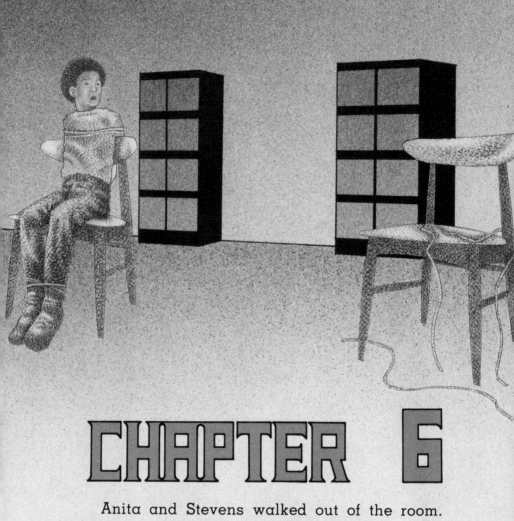

CHAPTER 6

Anita and Stevens walked out of the room. They closed the door behind them.

"I don't understand something," said Bobby. "Why would they rob their own store? And why hide the jewels in the wax museum?"

"Elementary," said Sherlock. "First of all, this is not their store. They just work here. And as for the jewels, they had to find a hiding place.

The wax museum is close by. Queen Victoria wears many jewels. They thought a few more would never be noticed. Now tell me," Sherlock asked. "Do you have such a thing as a telephone? They were quite new in my day."

"Of course," said Bobby. "There is one there on the desk."

Sherlock walked over to the phone.

"How did you get untied?" Bobby asked in surprise.

"An old trick," said Sherlock. "I'll teach it to you some day. But now we must call the police. How do you use this thing?"

"Dial zero," said Bobby. "Then ask for the police."

Sherlock got through to the police right away. "The great Sherlock Holmes here," he said. "I have the Circle Jewelry Store robbers. Meet me at the wax museum in 20 minutes. We will be in front of Queen Victoria." Sherlock

hung up. "It's all set," he said.

"Wait! How will we get the robbers back to the museum?" Bobby asked.

"I have a plan," said Sherlock. "As long as the police meet us, we have no worries." Sherlock jumped back into the chair. He tied his hands again.

Meanwhile, at the police station, everyone was laughing. "He must think we are stupid," laughed a police officer. "Imagine pretending to be Sherlock Holmes!" All the police officers laughed again.

CHAPTER 7

Anita and Stevens rushed into the room.

"All right, you two," said Anita. "Your time is up!"

Bobby looked scared. "Don't worry," Sherlock whispered. Then he began to laugh out loud.

"What is so funny?" Stevens barked.

"You," replied Sherlock. "You have lost your jewels for good. The Queen Victoria statue is being shipped out of the country tomorrow. And," he continued, "your jewels are leaving with her."

"Thank you for telling us," said Anita. "We

will just have to get them tonight."

"Not without our help," said Sherlock. He winked at Bobby. "I locked the back door. There is another way in. But only I know it."

"Then you will help us," Stevens said in a threatening voice.

"Very well," said Sherlock. "You leave me no choice." Once again he winked at the boy.

Anita untied Bobby and Sherlock. "This had better not be a trick," she said. "If it is, the kid gets it!"

Within minutes, they were back at the museum. Sherlock opened a side window. "This window has been broken for months," he whispered to Bobby. "Luckily, the museum people never fixed it."

Soon they had all crawled inside. Sherlock led the way to Queen Victoria. Stevens held Bobby tightly. As they approached the statue, Sherlock began shouting.

"All right, officers," he screamed. "Here are your robbers. Come and get them!"

Anita and Stevens froze. But no police appeared. "Now it's our turn to laugh," snarled Stevens. "Your little trick didn't work."

"Mr. Holmes," cried Bobby. "What happened? You said they would be here."

"I don't know," replied Sherlock. "But I think we are in trouble!"

CHAPTER 8

Bobby tried to pull away from Stevens. But the man was too strong. Anita took the jewels off of the statue of Queen Victoria. Meanwhile, Sherlock looked around. Each wax figure stood on its own stand.

"Of course," Sherlock thought to himself, as he looked at the statues. "That's the answer." Slowly, he moved toward a statue that was right near Bobby and Stevens. He gave it a shove. All at once, it began to topple. "Watch out!" Sherlock cried. Stevens jumped back. As he did, he let go of Bobby. "Run, Watson! Run!" shouted Sherlock. The boy did as he was told. Soon, he and Sherlock were racing through the museum.

"After them," Anita shouted. "We can't let them get away!" With that, the two crooks began chasing Sherlock and Bobby.

"We have to call the police!" Bobby yelled.

"I just did," Sherlock yelled back. "They will be here any minute."

"How could you have called them?" said Bobby. "I was watching you."

"No time to explain," Sherlock cried. "They are catching up to us. We had better split up.

You go that way. Good luck, Watson," Sherlock said. And then he was gone.

Bobby sped through room after room. He was playing hide-and-seek again. But this time it was for real! He ducked into the small room he had hidden in earlier. Then he crept under a table and waited. A few minutes passed. Suddenly he heard footsteps. He lifted his head to see who it was. But the table was too low. He hit his head hard. The blow knocked him out. The last thing Bobby saw was Stevens walking toward him.

CHAPTER 9

When Bobby opened his eyes, a police officer was standing beside him. "Are you all right?" he asked, helping Bobby up.

"Yes," said the boy. "But what happened? Where are the robbers?"

"On their way to being locked up," said the officer. He and Bobby walked to the front of the museum.

"But how did you know to come here?" asked the boy.

"Your friend, Mike," replied the police officer. "He got worried about you. So, he came to us."

"You mean you captured the robbers by accident!" exclaimed the boy.

"Not exactly," said the officer. "There is a silent alarm. It's hooked up to the station house. It rings when a statue is moved from its stand. We heard it go off while talking to your friend."

"So, that's why Sherlock pushed the statue," Bobby said.

"Who pushed it?" the officer asked.

"He did," Bobby said. He pointed to Sherlock.

"Come on," said the police officer. "That's only a wax figure."

"But he was alive a minute ago," said Bobby. "Really!"

"You must have hit your head pretty hard," said the officer. "Come! You will feel better outside. And no more playing in museums!" He began walking away.

Bobby looked at the figure of Sherlock Holmes. He kept staring at it. It didn't move. Then he touched the lump on the back of his head. "Maybe the police officer was right," he

said. "Maybe I dreamed the whole thing." He started walking out.

Then, suddenly, he smelled something strange. "Tobacco!" thought the boy. "And it's the same kind Sherlock was smoking!"

Bobby wheeled around. The wax figure of Sherlock was still standing in its place. But now, rising from its pipe, was a puff of white smoke.